This edition published by Parragon Books Ltd in 2017

Parragon Books Ltd
Chartist House
15–17 Trim Street
Bath BA1 1HA, UK
www.parragon.com

ISBN 978-1-4748-9098-4

Printed in China

PAWFECT BOOK OF STORIES

Three tales to enjoy ...

Pups Save a Pony
Pups Save Old Trusty
Pups and the Big Freeze

Bath • New York • Cologne • Melbourne • Delhi
Hong Kong • Shenzhen • Singapore

Pups Save a Pony

Ryder and the pups are in the PAW Patroller with Robo-dog. They're excited to be on their way to Julius and Julia's ranch for a camping trip.

Marshall has even packed a suitcase bursting with special marshmallow treats!

The PAW Patroller arrives at the ranch.

"Welcome pups!" say Julius and Julia. They introduce Priscilla the pony to the PAW Patrol. "She's a little bit skittish," warns Julius.

Ryder and the pups start
to set up camp.

"I knew my catapult would
come in handy," says Rocky.
He pings the PAW Patrol's
tents out one by one and
they spring open to make
a perfect campsite.

Just then, a butterfly lands
on Priscilla's head. She bursts
out of her pen in fright and
lands on one of the tents!

When night falls, Ryder gathers everyone around a campfire to tell ghost stories.

But later that night, Priscilla hears a spooky noise. She doesn't know that it's only Julia and Julius being silly, and she bolts out of her pen into the desert!

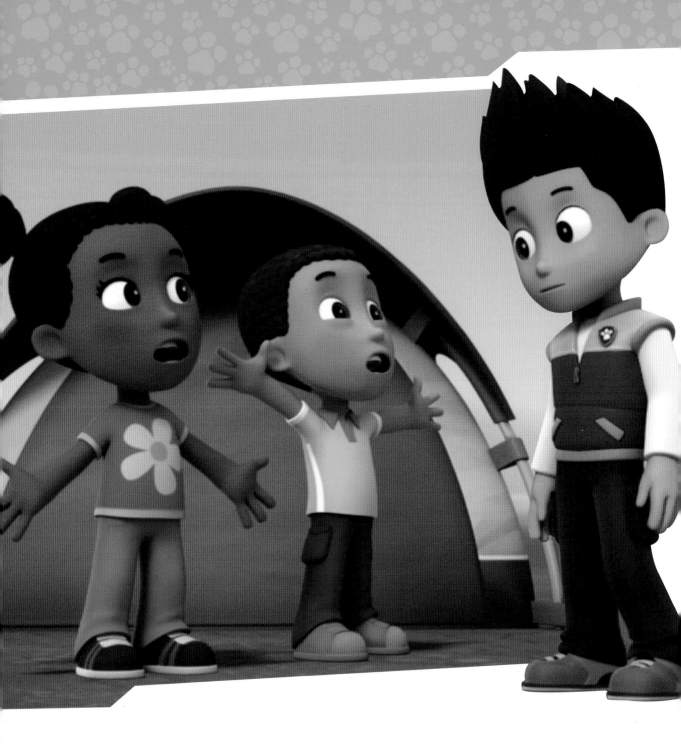

In the morning, Julia and Julius can't find Priscilla.
"We've looked everywhere!" they tell Ryder.

"Oh no! We'd better find her – and fast," replies Ryder.
"No ranch is too big, no job is too small!"

Ryder calls the pups to the PAW Patroller.

"PAW Patrol ready for action, Ryder, sir," barks Chase.

Ryder tells the pups the bad news that Priscilla has gone missing.

"It's too dangerous for Priscilla to be out on her own without food and water," explains Ryder. "We're going to start by looking for hoofprints."

Ryder needs Chase's nose to find the scent of Priscilla's trail and his truck to reach her fast. He also needs Skye to search from the air.

PAW Patrol is on a roll!

Ryder and Chase follow Skye as she soars over the desert following Priscilla's hoofprints. But soon the hoofprints disappear! The wind has blown dust over them.

"Chase, you and your nose are up next," says Ryder.

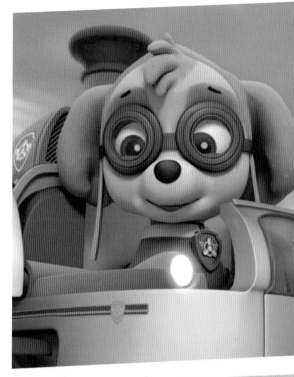

Chase uses his spy-nose to pick up Priscilla's scent.

"Ryder, I smell pony," says Chase. "Priscilla definitely went this way."

Chase leads the search party further into the desert.

Skye spots more hoofprints –
the trail leads to the edge of a canyon.

"Ryder, I've found her!" says Skye. "She's fallen down
a ravine." She swoops down and lands beside Priscilla.

"We're on our way," replies Ryder.

When Ryder and Chase arrive at the scene, Priscilla is trying to climb out of the ravine. But it's too steep for her. She's also too big for Skye's rescue harness!

Ryder picks up his PupPad.
"Rubble, we need you!"

"Rubble on the double," he barks.

Rubble zooms off to help rescue
Priscilla. Robo-dog drives the
PAW Patroller behind him.

"Thanks for hurrying, Rubble," says Ryder.
"The ravine is too steep for Priscilla to climb
out of, so I need you to dig a staircase to
help her."

"I'm on it – step by step," replies Rubble.

Rubble barks to activate his shovel.
He scoops out the earth to make the first step.

"Great work, Rubble," says Ryder.

"Thanks! I dig digging," replies Rubble.

Rubble quickly digs a perfect staircase, but Priscilla doesn't know how to climb stairs!

Ryder has an idea. "Chase, we need your zip line," he says.

"Yes, sir, Ryder," replies Chase.

Ryder zooms across the zip line. "This is the fun part," he says. "YEEHAW!"

He makes a neat landing on Priscilla's back!

"Good catch, Priscilla," says Ryder.

Ryder guides Priscilla up the staircase and to the top of the ravine.

"Good pony," says Skye.

With Priscilla rescued, Robo Dog pulls up in the PAW Patroller to drive everyone back to the ranch.

Suddenly, a butterfly flutters into the PAW Patroller and distracts Robo-dog. He starts pressing all the wrong controls! The PAW Patroller's wheels spin in the desert sand and it slides to the edge of the ravine.

"Oh no! The PAW Patroller is stuck!" says Ryder.

The pups try to move it with Chase's winch, but the PAW Patroller does not budge.

"Looks like we're going to need a few more helping paws," says Ryder.

The rest of the pups rush to the rescue, but even when they work together they can't move the PAW Patroller.

"We don't have enough horsepower," says Chase.

Ryder thinks for a moment. "Who needs horsepower when we have pony power?" he says.

Zuma throws Priscilla his lifebuoy and she helps pull the PAW Patroller to safety!

That evening, everyone
is happy to be back
at the camp.

"Phew! What an
adventure," says Julia.
"Thanks, Ryder."

"Thank Priscilla! She saved the
day," replies Ryder. "If we're
in trouble, we'll yelp for help!"

Pups Save
Old Trusty

Today, Jake and Everest are on Jake's Mountain showing around a visiting family. The next stop on their tour is Old Trusty.

"Old Trusty is a geyser," explains Jake. "Water builds up under the ground and then *WHOOSH!* – it shoots out in a big wet jet."

With a rumble and a shudder the geyser does just that!

Suddenly, there's another, much louder, rumble and the ground begins to shake!

"That's not a geyser," says Everest, "that's a rockslide!"

The boulders crash down the mountain and everyone runs underneath a cliff to get out of the way.

The rockslide is soon over but the fallen boulders have blocked the way out from under the cliff!

"We're going to need help," says Jake. He looks for his phone but it got lost in the rockslide. So did Everest's PupPad!

"Don't worry folks," says Jake. "Everest will go and get help."

Everest barks out her grappling hook and begins to climb the boulders.

"Wow! Look at her go," says the dad.

Everest makes it over to the other side and sets off to find help.

Everest arrives at her Pup House and it transforms into a snowplough.

"Off the trail, Everest won't fail!"

She zooms off to find the rest of the PAW Patrol.

Meanwhile, Mayor Goodway and Chickaletta are enjoying an ice cream sundae when a water jet suddenly shoots them into the air!

They land on the roof of City Hall. "The views up here are breathtaking," says Major Goodway, "but this is a breathtaking disaster!"

She calls Ryder for help.

"Hi, Mayor Goodway," says Ryder. "What's up?"

"I am, Ryder! And Chickaletta, too," the mayor replies. "A mysterious jet of water whooshed us up to the top of City Hall. Water jets are popping up all over town!"

"We'll be right there," Ryder replies.

Ryder calls the PAW Patrol to the Lookout. When they arrive, the pups line up for action.

Ryder explains that Mayor Goodway is stranded on the roof of City Hall because strange jets of water have been popping up all over town.

"We're going to help the mayor down first and then find out what's been causing the jets," says Ryder.

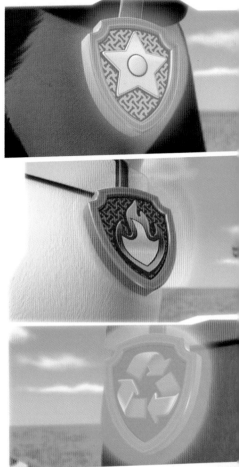

"Skye, I need you and your harness to rescue the mayor," says Ryder. "Rubble, I need you and your crane to lift the bench off the roof."

"Rubble on the double!" barks the construction pup.

"PAW Patrol is on a roll!" says Ryder.

Skye, Rubble and Ryder arrive at City Hall.

Skye lowers her harness to Mayor Goodway and Chickaletta. Mayor Goodway bravely reaches out for the harness, even though she's scared. "We can do it. We can do it," she says.

"Yes! You did it," says Skye, carrying them to safety.

Next, Rubble barks out his crane. He carefully lowers the bench down to the ground.

Just then, Everest arrives at City Hall. She tells Ryder that Jake and the visiting family are trapped on Jake's Mountain.

"We have to go and help Jake," Ryder tells Rubble and Skye. "Then we'll find out what's been causing these water jets."

Ryder and the pups arrive at Jake's Mountain. The fallen boulders make everything look so different that Everest can't remember where Jake and the family are trapped!

"We need some air surveillance," says Ryder.

"Got it, Ryder," replies Skye.

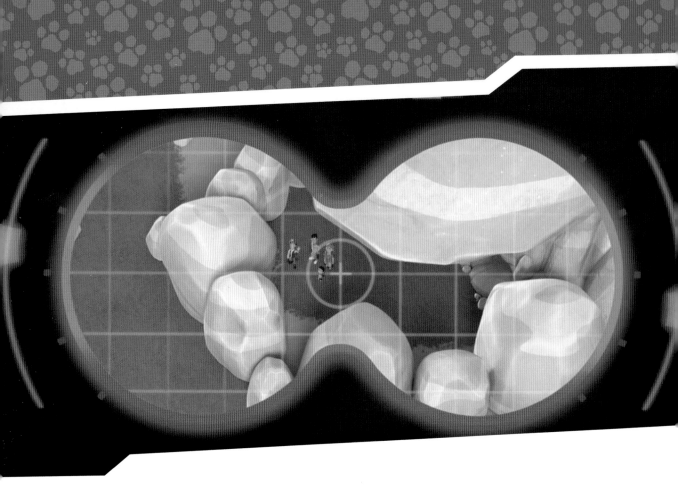

Skye soars up into the air and uses her goggles to find Jake and the family. Ryder, Rubble and Everest race over to help them.

"Rubble, let's get that rock rolling," says Ryder.

"Time to put the shove in shovel," replies Rubble.
He uses his giant shovel to move a heavy boulder.
Jake and the family are finally free!

"Thanks! That was one tight spot," says Jake.

RUMBLE, RUMBLE! The ground shakes again, but this time it sounds like Old Trusty.

"Something's not right," says Jake, worried.

Everyone races off to Old Trusty and finds that a giant boulder has blocked the water flow!

"So that's why water has been shooting up everywhere," says Ryder. "If Old Trusty's blocked, the water needs to find another way to get out."

Rubble and Everest work together to try and move the boulder blocking poor Old Trusty.

But the boulder won't budge.

"If we all work together when the geyser erupts it will give us a super boost," says Ryder.

Everyone lines up behind Everest and Rubble, and waits for Old Trusty to rumble.

Suddenly, the water roars beneath the boulder.

"This is it, everybody," says Ryder. "PUSH!"

With all their strength, everyone gives the boulder one last push and *POP!* the boulder finally shoots up into the air.

"The pups saved Old Trusty for us," says the
little girl. "Thanks PAW Patrol!"

"You're welcome," says Ryder. "The PAW Patrol
is here to help!"

Pups and the Big Freeze

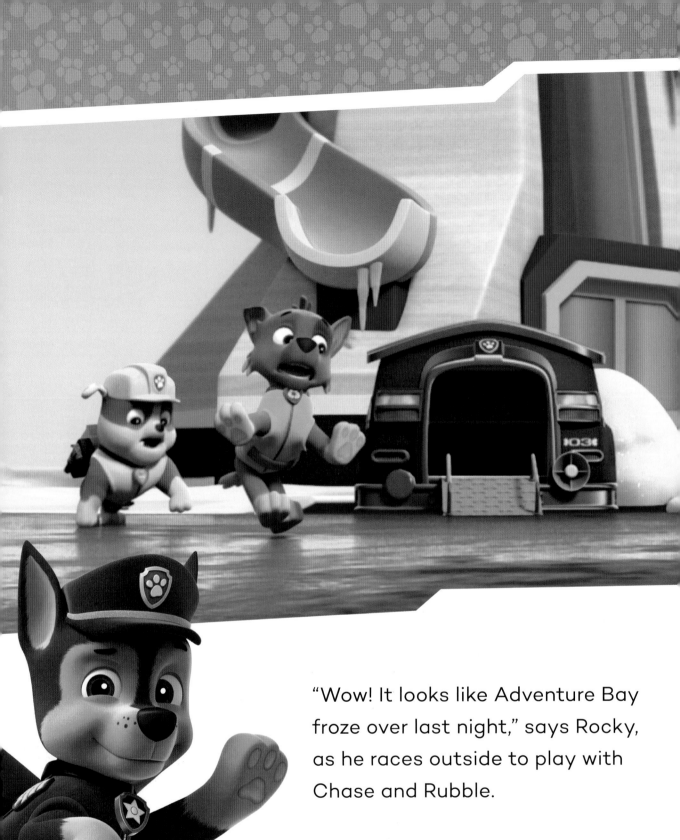

"Wow! It looks like Adventure Bay froze over last night," says Rocky, as he races outside to play with Chase and Rubble.

"Whoaaa!" cry the pups, skidding across the icy ground into ...

... a huge pile of snow!

"It really did freeze last night," says
Chase, giggling at their new snow hats.

Over near the bridge, Mayor Goodway and Chickaletta are sliding around on the ice, too.

"Oh no!" Mayor Goodway cries, as her car skates across the icy road and crashes into a big bank of snow.

"I'm stuck!" says the mayor, trying to reverse out. "I need to call the PAW Patrol."

"Ryder," says Mayor Goodway over the phone, "the streets are covered in ice and my car slid into a bank of snow. I can't get out."

"Leave it to the pups, Mayor Goodway,"
Ryder replies. "We're on our way."

Ryder hits the alarm on the PupPad
and says, "PAW Patrol to the Lookout!"

"PAW Patrol, ready for action!" says Chase when all the pups arrive.

"Thanks, pups," says Ryder. "Adventure Bay is super-slippery today. Mayor Goodway slid into a snow bank and she needs our help."

Ryder asks Chase to bring his winch,
then tells Rubble to clear the roads.

"Rubble on the double!" says
the pup, taking the lead and
clearing the way with
his digger.

"Great job, Rubble," says Ryder when they reach Mayor Goodway. "Chase – it's winch time."

"Chase is on the case!" replies the police pup.

Ryder ties the winch on to Mayor Goodway's car and Chase starts his police truck's motor.

The winch pulls the car out of the snow.

"Well done, Chase," says Ryder. "All clear, Mayor Goodway."

"Thank you for rescuing me," says the mayor.

Just then, Ryder's PupPad rings. It's the train driver.

"Branches are blocking the crossing," he says. "And the train's brakes won't work on the icy tracks!"

"We're on it!" says Ryder.

"I know just the pup
to lend a paw," says Ryder.
He calls husky pup Everest.

"Hello, Ryder. How can
I help?" Everest asks.

"The train crossing
is blocked and we have
to clear the tracks," says Ryder.
"Come quickly!"

"Ice or snow, I'm ready to go!" says Everest, hopping into her snowplough.

She drives along the mountain road towards the train crossing.

"The train driver can't stop," explains Ryder when Everest arrives. "And if he hits the fallen branches, the train will jump the track. We have to work quickly."

Leaping into action, Chase and Ryder use the winch to pull the branches off the track.

"Winch hook!" barks Chase.

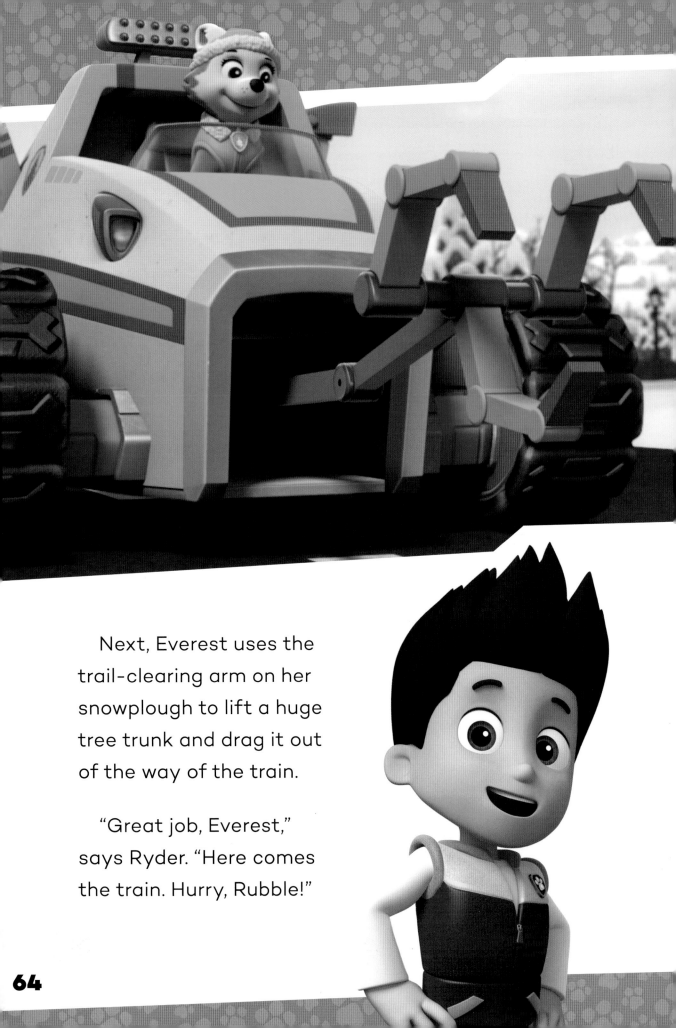

Next, Everest uses the trail-clearing arm on her snowplough to lift a huge tree trunk and drag it out of the way of the train.

"Great job, Everest," says Ryder. "Here comes the train. Hurry, Rubble!"

Rubble pushes his shovel along the tracks, scraping the ice and snow away as fast as he can.

When the train approaches the station, Ryder tells Rubble to pull over.

The train driver puts on the brakes and comes to a stop at the station. *HONK! HONK!*

"Woo-hoo! The brakes are holding," says the train driver. "Thanks, Rubble!"

"No problem," Rubble replies.

"We did it!" says Ryder, heading back to the bridge to meet everyone. "Now let's celebrate. Who wants to skate?"

"I was born to slide!" says Everest, and she and the rest of the pups race off to play.

"This will help you slide, Everest!" cries Marshall. "Water cannon!" The pup shoots a stream of water that instantly freezes into an arch in the cold air.

"An ice slide!" says Everest, scrambling to the top. She zooms down so fast that she bumps into Zuma and Skye at the bottom. "Whoooaaa!"

The pups all go flying up, up, up … and straight into a pile of snow!

"Hee, hee, hee!" everyone laughs, looking at their silly snow hats.

"What a good bunch of pups," says Ryder.